Woooo!

For Helen and Frieda

W₀₀₀₀!

A HUTCHINSON BOOK 978 0 857 54022 5

Published in Great Britain by Hutchinson,
a division of Random House Children's Publishers UK
A Random House Group Company

This edition published 2014

13 5 7 9 10 8 6 4 2

Copyright © Gerry Turley, 2014

The right of Gerry Turley to be identified as the author and illustrator of this work has been asserted
in accordance with the Copyright, Designs and Patents Act 1988.

RANDOM HOUSE CHILDREN'S PUBLISHERS UK
61–63 Uxbridge Road, London W5 5SA

www.randomhousechildrens.co.uk
www.randomhouse.co.uk

Addresses for companies within The Random House Group Limited can be found at: www.randomhouse.co.uk/offices.htm

THE RANDOM HOUSE GROUP Limited Reg. No. 954009

A CIP catalogue record for this book is available from the British Library.

Printed in China

The Random House Group Limited supports the Forest Stewardship Council® (FSC®), the leading international
forest-certification organisation. Our books carrying the FSC label are printed on FSC®-certified paper.
FSC is the only forest-certification scheme supported by the leading environmental organisations,
including Greenpeace. Our paper procurement policy can be found at
www.randomhouse.co.uk/environment.

MIX
Paper from
responsible sources
FSC
www.fsc.org   FSC® C104723

Woooo!

Gerry Turley

In the wild wild woods two hungry babies wait for lunch.

squeak

You're ready to fly, little ones.

flap

Flap your wings.

flop

flump

swoosh

whoosh

Into the **wild** **wild** **wild** **woods** . . .

nosssssssshh

gnash gnash

meep

He was all alone with danger creeping closer.

Scre

And the little
owl began
to fly . . .

woo-hoo

and went
up, up
and away!

Flap
Flap

Woooo

As high as
the moon . . .